Silver Dolphins

RIVER RESCUE

For Lizzie Ryley

www.summerwaters.co.uk

First published in paperback by HarperCollins *Children's Books* in 2010

HarperCollins *Children's Books* is a division of HarperCollins *Publishers* Ltd,
77-85 Fulham Palace Road, Hammersmith, London W6 8JB.

Visit our website at: www.harpercollins.co.uk

2
ISBN: 978-0-00-736750-4

Typeset by Palimpsest Book Production Limited,
Falkirk, Stirlingshire

Printed and bound in England by Clays Ltd, St Ives plc

by **Summer Waters**

Silver Dolphins
RIVER RESCUE

HarperCollins *Children's Books*

Prologue

A group of dolphins were playing follow my leader along the seabed. In and out of the rocks they chased each other in a long, wiggly line.

"It's my turn to be leader now," clicked Swift, one of the older dolphins.

Swift swam fast, weaving between the rocks, turning somersaults and rolling in the water. The dolphins chased after him, squealing with delight.

"This is so much fun!" exclaimed Bubbles.

"Let's go and play in the kelp beds," said Swift. "That'll be even more fun."

"Bubbly," clicked Bubbles. "You lead and we'll follow."

But as Swift headed out to sea, a tiny dolphin named Dot called from the back, "Mum doesn't let me go to the kelp beds on my own."

"You're not on your own. You're with us," said Swift.

Dot stopped swimming and shook her head. "Sorry, but I'm not allowed to go there without a grown-up. Please can we play here?"

"I'm going to the kelp beds," said Swift firmly. "Stay here if you don't want to come."

"But I won't have anyone to play with," squeaked Dot.

"I'll stay behind with you," said Bubbles.

He darted out of the line and swam over to her.

"You said you'd go to the kelp beds," said Swift crossly. "You can't just change your mind."

"I can," said Bubbles.

"Well, I'm not changing mine," said Swift crossly. "Follow me, everyone."

The other dolphins hesitated, then some followed Swift and some stayed with Bubbles and Dot. They immediately started a new game, unaware that Spirit and Star were watching them.

"Bubbles was right," said Star proudly. "You *can* change your mind."

Spirit uttered a long sigh. "If only all choices were that simple. I sense much harder decisions ahead for the Silver Dolphins."

"Can we help them?" asked Star.

"No," said Spirit sadly. "The Silver Dolphins must choose for themselves."

Chapter One

ntonia Lee woke with the sun on her face and a wonderful feeling bubbling inside her. It was the first day of the spring holiday. Two whole weeks of fun and spending as much time as she liked helping at Sea Watch, the marine conservation charity run by her friend Cai's great-aunt Claudia. Hurriedly, Antonia

washed and dressed then went downstairs for breakfast.

Mum and Dad were drinking tea in the kitchen.

"You're up early," said Dad. "Did you forget there was no school?"

"I'm going to Sea Watch," said Antonia, pouring herself a bowl of cereal. "There's a lot to do because it's just volunteers today – Cai and Claudia aren't there this morning."

"Of course!" exclaimed Mum, passing Antonia a mug of tea. "They'll be on their way to the airport to collect Cai's parents."

Cai was living with his great-aunt Claudia in Sandy Bay because his mum and dad had temporary jobs in Australia.

"How long are they over here for?" asked Dad.

"Ten days," said Antonia. She finished her breakfast then sat on the kitchen floor to put on her trainers.

"Are you coming back for lunch?" Mum stepped over her to get to the dishwasher.

"No, I made some sandwiches last night. I'll be home for tea, though." Antonia's voice trailed away as a very familiar feeling swept over her. It made her tingle with anticipation. The dolphins needed her! Any minute now the silver dolphin charm Antonia always wore round her neck would call her to the sea.

"Got to go," she said, hurriedly jumping up. "See you later."

"Have a good day," called Mum.

As Antonia closed the front door her silver dolphin charm vibrated and its tiny tail tapped against her neck. The charm was as soft as a

real dolphin. Antonia shivered with delight as suddenly a high-pitched whistle that only a Silver Dolphin could hear shrilled from it.

Silver Dolphin, we need you.

Spirit, I hear your call, Antonia silently answered as she headed towards the beach.

Both Antonia and Cai were Silver Dolphins, or guardians of the sea. They had special magical abilities that let them swim and communicate with dolphins! With these amazing abilities came the responsibility to care for sea life. Antonia wished that Cai was there too as she ran towards Gull Bay. He'd be frustrated that he'd missed Spirit's call, even though he was really excited about meeting his parents at the airport. Antonia jumped down on to the deserted beach. The soft, white sand shifted beneath her feet as

River Rescue

she ran over to the rocks. Pulling off her trainers and socks, Antonia left them under a rock and ran down to the sea. The water was chilly and her teeth chattered as she waded deeper. There were goose bumps on her arms and legs, but Antonia kept walking. When the sea was deep enough she gracefully dived in. The water was so cold it made her gasp, but she quickly warmed up as her legs melded together to kick like a dolphin's tail. Hands paddling like flippers, body arching in and out of the sea, Antonia swam to find Spirit.

It wasn't long before she saw four silver heads in the water. Antonia swam on, pleased that Spirit had brought his family – Star, Dream and Bubbles – with him. She greeted Spirit first, rubbing her nose against his. Bubbles impatiently bobbed in the water, waiting for

his turn, then greeted Antonia enthusiastically.

"Thank you for answering our call, Silver Dolphin," said Spirit. "Bubbles and Dream have found an old fishing net on the seabed."

"Show me where," said Antonia at once. Lost or abandoned fishing nets posed a serious threat to sea life. If animals got stuck in them they either starved or drowned.

"Follow me," said Bubbles importantly.

Antonia dived under the sea and swam after Bubbles, with Spirit, Star and Dream following.

"There," said Bubbles, pointing with his nose.

"Don't get too close," Spirit clicked in warning as Bubbles swam nearer.

The net was like a hideous brown monster slumbering on the seabed. Antonia swam round it, her eyes quickly sliding over the rotting fish and the dead starfish trapped in

its squares. It was large and would be awkward to carry, but she thought she could manage it on her own. Fighting back her revulsion, Antonia pulled the dead creatures away then carefully folded the net in half and rolled it into a bundle.

"Stay back," she warned as Bubbles inched closer to see what she was doing.

Antonia scooped the net up and swam upwards until her head broke through the water's surface.

"Phew," she panted. "It's heavy."

"When he arrives the other Silver Dolphin will help you get it ashore," said Bubbles confidently.

"He's not coming," said Antonia. "He's gone to meet his parents. They've come back from Australia to visit him."

"That's lovely. He must really miss them," clicked Star sympathetically.

"He does," said Antonia.

Bubbles looked scared. "What if he decides to go and live in Australia with his parents?" he asked.

Antonia laughed and said confidently, "That won't happen. Cai loves it here. Being a Silver Dolphin is the best thing that's ever happened to him."

The net was weighing her down so she headed to shore. The dolphins swam with her, clicking encouragement but not offering any help – nets were too dangerous. Soon Antonia was red in the face with exertion.

"Not far now," she panted as the beach drew closer.

"Can the Silver Dolphin come back and play

when she's taken the net ashore?" asked Bubbles hopefully.

"Yes, if she'd like to," clicked Spirit.

Antonia shook her head sadly. "I'd love to, but I can't. I'm needed at Sea Watch today. I'll play another time."

Bubbles looked disappointed as he said goodbye, splashing his tail in the water.

Antonia headed straight for the beach. When it was shallow enough to paddle, she dumped the net in the surf while she caught her breath. Sea water poured from her clothes like a miniature waterfall, leaving everything as dry as if she'd never been in the water. Antonia ran her hand through her long, blonde hair, straightening out a few damp tangles. A nasty odour was coming from the net. Antonia wrinkled her nose and, holding it carefully

away from her, carried it up the beach and fed it into the dustbin. If Cai had been there to help she would have taken the net back to the Sea Watch bin rather than fill the one on the beach, but it was too heavy and smelly to carry to Sea Watch on her own.

Antonia put on her shoes and socks, chuckling as she remembered Bubbles's comment about Cai returning to live with his parents. Cai was very excited about seeing his mum and dad, but there was no way he'd go back to Australia with them. His world was here in Sandy Bay. Thinking about the fun times they'd had together, Antonia hurried to Sea Watch.

Chapter Two

It felt funny going to Sea Watch, knowing that neither Cai or Claudia would be there. The door was unlocked, but the building had an empty feel to it.

"Hello, is anyone here?" called Antonia.

"Hi, Antonia, I'm in the back room," Sally, an adult volunteer who took charge when Claudia was away, called out.

Antonia opened the door and found Sally sitting on a chair, feeding a fox cub with a baby's bottle.

"You're early," Sally said, smiling at Antonia.

"Not as early as you," said Antonia, smiling back. "Oh, how sweet! When did the fox cub come in?"

"This is Rusty. A motorist brought him in last night. His mother was killed by a car. The motorist found him lying next to her at the side of the road."

Antonia stood very still, watching the cub suck lethargically from the bottle of milk. He had chocolate-coloured fur, large ears and a tiny black nose.

"He's so cute," she whispered.

Rusty couldn't finish the bottle. Sally

looked worried as she put him back in his pen.

"I'll try him again later," she said, shutting the door.

Rusty settled down with his nose in his tail and closed his eyes.

"Maybe he's tired," said Antonia.

"Let's hope so. He had quite a traumatic night. Claudia said he was terrified when he first arrived. Poor Claudia! She was up half the night dealing with Rusty, so she didn't get much sleep before she had to get up and go to the airport."

Sally poured Rusty's milk down the sink and washed the bottle.

"What do you want me to do today?" asked Antonia.

"The razorbill and the herring gulls need

cleaning out and feeding, but if that's too much for you I could find something easier?"

"I'll do the birds," said Antonia, pleased to be busy. Sea Watch felt weird without Claudia and Cai. It was far too quiet and empty. Antonia hoped that some other volunteers would arrive soon. Putting on a disposable apron and a pair of gloves, she collected cleaning materials and went outside to the aviaries. The first one contained Billy the razorbill, who was recovering from getting oil on his feathers. He sat on a perch watching Antonia navigate the porch with its double-door system designed to stop birds escaping.

"Urr," he said conversationally.

"Urr," answered Antonia, mimicking his throaty growl.

She removed the soiled straw from his sleeping quarters and replaced it with a fresh batch. Then she cleaned out his water bowl and refilled it. After that, Antonia swept and mopped the concrete floor. Finally, she left Billy with a fish breakfast and went outside to sweep round the aviary, clearing away the bits of straw and bird seed.

"Hi, Antonia."

Antonia was so engrossed in her job that she hadn't heard Emily arrive.

"Do you need any help?"

"Yes, please," said Antonia. "I'm just about to start on the gulls."

It was fun working with Emily. She made Antonia laugh telling her stories about life in Year Seven at Sandy Bay High, the local comprehensive. They finished the gulls in half

the time it had taken Antonia to do Billy and then went inside. To Antonia's surprise it was mid-morning and time to stop for a break. She sat with Sally and the other volunteers and was drinking squash and eating a biscuit when Cai arrived back from the airport with his parents and Claudia.

"Everyone, this is my mum and dad," announced Cai, pinching a biscuit from the plate.

Antonia had met Cai's parents before, but hadn't seen them for ages and was overcome with shyness. She quickly recovered when Mr and Mrs Pacific hugged her warmly.

"How was your flight?" she asked, hugging them back.

"Good," said Mr Pacific, "until we stepped off the plane and remembered how cold it is

here in April." He shivered dramatically and chattered his teeth.

"This isn't cold, it's warm!" exclaimed Cai.

Mr and Mrs Pacific looked as sleepy as Rusty the fox cub after their long flight, but Cai was too excited to notice and insisted on showing them round with Antonia.

"Come and see outside," he said, after they'd looked at everything indoors. "We've got new aviaries, a deepwater pool and our own beach."

"Is it the same beach that was here the last time I visited Claudia?" Mr Pacific joked.

Cai laughed. "You haven't seen the deepwater pool, though," he said persuasively.

"We'll see the outside later, honey," said Mrs Pacific, smothering a yawn with her hand. "Right now I need to lie down before I fall down!"

Antonia didn't go up to the house with Cai. Expecting him to stay with his parents, she went down to the beach with Emily to take some sea-water samples. But it wasn't long before Cai joined them.

"That was quick," said Antonia.

"There wasn't much point in hanging around," said Cai. "Mum and Dad are having a sleep in Claudia's spare room."

"Don't you miss your parents?" asked Emily curiously. "I'd miss mine if they lived on the other side of the world."

Cai sighed. "I do miss them loads, but when we all lived together I didn't see them much because they were working such long hours. In a way, it's better like this. Now when I see them they take time off work so we can do stuff together. Dad's taking me

windsurfing and he said you could come too, Antonia."

"Really? I've always wanted to try that," said Antonia enthusiastically. She was pleased Mr Pacific had invited her.

There was so much to do at Sea Watch that the day sped by. Claudia was concerned about Rusty, who still wasn't feeding well, and she rang Mr Singh, the vet, for a chat. She looked a little happier afterwards.

"Mr Singh thinks our cub might be cold. He told me to put a heat lamp in his pen and see if that helps. He's also suggested getting in touch with the Sandy Bay Badger Sanctuary. They take in injured or orphaned fox cubs as well as badgers, so I'm going to see if they have room for Rusty. Mr Singh thinks he'll be much better off there because they have lots

of experience dealing with young cubs. They'll have other foxes for Rusty to socialise with."

At the end of the day Antonia and Cai couldn't resist going to visit the cub before they went home. Rusty looked so small and cute curled up in the pen on his own.

"I wish we could keep him here until he's big enough to release back into the wild," said Cai.

"Me too," Antonia agreed. "But it wouldn't be fair. He'll be much happier at the badger sanctuary."

"I wonder if he misses his parents," said Cai with a soft sigh.

Antonia gave Cai a look as he headed for the door.

But Cai sounded his usual cheery self as he called back, "See you tomorrow, Antonia. And

don't forget to ask if you can go windsurfing
while my parents are here."

"I'll ask as soon as I get in," said Antonia,
following him.

Chapter Three

The moment Antonia arrived home her little sister Jessica swooped on her.

"Come and play with me," she said. "I've built a den in my bedroom with blankets and pegs. It's really cool."

"In a minute, Jess," said Antonia. She wanted to ask Mum about going windsurfing first.

"That was nice of Cai's dad," said Mum. "Of course you can go."

"Good, now you can come and play with me," said Jessica.

Laughing good-naturedly, Antonia let Jessica pull her upstairs.

"Close your eyes," said Jessica bossily.

Antonia closed them and Jess flung open her bedroom door, declaring dramatically, "Open them again."

"Wow!" exclaimed Antonia. "This is really cool, Jess."

The den took up most of the bedroom and reminded Antonia of a Bedouin tent in the desert. It was built from blankets pegged to various objects in the room. There was a string of pink and blue flower-shaped lights hanging around the entrance. The bedroom curtains

were drawn and the lights glowed prettily in the darkened room. Antonia crawled inside and found that the den was comfortably furnished with cushions and pillows. The bathroom radio was playing softly in the background and Jessica had put a framed photo of Mum, Dad and Antonia on a table made from an upside-down box.

"I love it," said Antonia, settling on a cushion.

They only had a short time to play before tea, so after they'd eaten, Jessica asked Antonia if she'd come back to the den to play some more.

"Not tonight," said Mum, stacking the dirty plates. "It's time to take the den down and get in the bath."

"Can I leave it up?" asked Jess. "I want to

play in it again tomorrow. Antonia does too, don't you?"

"I'd love to, but I'm going to Sea Watch," said Antonia. "I'll play with you when I get home, though."

"Is that a good idea when you're going windsurfing with Cai?" asked Mum. "I thought you might give Sea Watch a break for a day or two. Cai's not seen his parents for ages and he might like some time alone with them."

"Then Cai won't come to Sea Watch, he'll stay up at the house," said Antonia reasonably.

Dad sighed wistfully. "Lucky you! Before I started my garage business I used to go windsurfing. Those were the days... when I had time for hobbies!"

Antonia groaned loudly. It was a family joke

that Dad never had time for anything because he was always working.

"Just don't overstay your welcome," said Mum. "Cai's a good friend. He might not tell you that he doesn't want you around all the time in case he hurts your feelings."

"Cai knows me better than that!" said Antonia indignantly. "We don't have secrets from each other."

"What about my den?" Jessica interrupted. "Can I keep it up or not?"

Mum hesitated. "All right, but no more playing in it tonight. Go and get in the bath." Mum followed Jessica upstairs to get her a towel from the airing cupboard.

Antonia went outside and stared at the bay. The blue sea shimmered invitingly and she longed to be swimming in it. She

screwed up her eyes against the slanting evening sunshine, hoping she might see her dolphins. But the only things in the water were the bright-green canoes of the Sandy Bay rowing club. Disappointed, Antonia went indoors.

The next morning, Antonia was the first volunteer to arrive at Sea Watch. Claudia was pleased to see her and handed her a warm bottle of milk, saying, "Can you feed Rusty for me?"

"I'd love to," said Antonia.

"Great," said Claudia. "I need to put in an order for supplies and if I don't do it now we're going to run out of things. Please can you make a note of how much milk he drinks? He took a little more last night, but it's still

not as much as he should be having. His record sheet is by the pen."

"I'll do that. Where's Cai?" asked Antonia as she pulled on a pair of disposable gloves.

"Cai's having breakfast with his mum and dad. He'll be down later." There was a catch in Claudia's voice, and Antonia looked at her in surprise.

"Is everything all right?"

"Yes." Claudia abruptly began rummaging in the cupboard, giving Antonia the strong impression she was hiding something. Remembering the conversation she had with her mum, Antonia suddenly felt uncomfortable. What if Mum was right? What if Cai didn't want her around now that his parents were back?

"There you go." Claudia backed out of the

cupboard and handed a towel to Antonia.

"You know the drill," she said, smiling warmly. "Sit Rusty on this when you feed him so you don't spoil your clothes."

Claudia sounded normal again so Antonia decided she must have been imagining things.

"Thanks." Taking the towel in one hand and the milk in the other, Antonia went to the back room to feed Rusty.

The cub was a little livelier today, but he took a while to latch on to the bottle and he didn't finish the milk. Antonia sat patiently, wiggling the bottle to encourage the cub to drink more. It was peaceful in the back room. Sun streamed through the window, warming Antonia's face and making Rusty's coat gleam like molten chocolate. Her thoughts wandered to Cai. She was surprised that he was still

having breakfast. Cai was an early riser. He must have waited to eat with his mum and dad.

When it was obvious that Rusty wasn't going to take any more milk, Antonia put him back in his pen. The cub clung to her, but Antonia was firm.

"I'm not allowed to cuddle you," she said, pushing his paws away. "Sorry, but it's for your own good."

Antonia wrote down the amount of milk Rusty had drunk on his record sheet, then emptied the remainder down the sink. She washed the empty bottle and soaked it in sterilising solution. There was still no sign of Cai and none of the other volunteers had arrived either. As Antonia collected the things she needed to clean out Billy and the gull's

aviaries, she wondered whether she should have stayed away too.

"Thank goodness you're here," said Claudia, suddenly looking up from her computer. "I would never have managed on my own."

Antonia smiled gratefully. She knew Claudia meant it. They were good at reading each other's minds. Feeling much more cheerful, Antonia went outside to the birds. As she reached the aviary she heard footsteps behind her.

"Antonia!"

Antonia was pleased to see Cai and waited for him to catch her up.

"Hi, sorry I'm late. Mum and Dad took ages to get up this morning." Cai's smile didn't quite reach his eyes as he opened Billy's aviary door for her. Arms full of mop, bucket and

cleaning things, Antonia went inside. Cai squeezed in after her and when he'd shut the outer door, Antonia opened the inner one.

"I thought you might not come today," she said.

"Why? Cos my parents are here? It's brilliant having them around, but we don't have to do everything together."

"I wouldn't mind if you did."

"Well, I don't," said Cai forcefully.

Surprised at Cai's snappy tone, Antonia started cleaning Billy's cage. She and Cai worked in silence until the razorbill cocked his head and said cheekily, "Urrr!"

Antonia and Cai burst out laughing.

"You cheeky thing!" said Cai.

With the silence broken, Cai began telling Antonia a funny story about his dad falling asleep

at dinner and getting strawberry cheesecake in his hair. Antonia giggled appreciatively. But deep down she was convinced that Cai wasn't as cheerful as he sounded. There was a worry line on his forehead and his brown eyes had lost their usual sparkle. By the time they'd finished Billy's cage and cleaned out the gulls, Antonia couldn't bear it any longer.

"Is everything all right?" she asked.

"It's fine," said Cai briskly.

At once, Antonia knew it wasn't. It wasn't like Cai to be so short. Her mind whirled with reasons that would explain his strange mood, but only one held fast. Cai had realised he was missing his parents more than he was letting on. Then another thought struck Antonia. What if he wanted to go back to Australia and live with them?

That's mad. Antonia dismissed the idea immediately. Cai had been living with his great-aunty Claudia for ten months and he'd never once mentioned that he missed his parents enough to want to go and live in Australia. But ten months was a long time. Maybe he'd had enough of only seeing his parents in the holidays.

"You missed a bit," said Cai, breaking into her thoughts. "Here, give me the mop. I'll do it. You're miles away."

Cai often teased Antonia for being dreamy, but this time he sounded different. Not liking his bossy tone, she shook her head and carried on sluicing water on the floor.

"Come on," said Cai irritably. "We haven't got all day. There's a ton of other things to do."

"Well, go and do them," said Antonia pointedly.

She regretted the words the instant she spoke. Cai opened his mouth to reply, then shaking his head he left the aviary and began sweeping the path in front of it. Antonia felt awful. She violently scrubbed the aviary floor with the mop as if she could scrub out the hurt feeling gnawing at her stomach. She was so intent on her work that she almost didn't notice another, nicer, sensation stealing over her.

Suddenly, Antonia stood up and pushed her hair away from her face. Spirit was about to call. As the feeling welled up inside her, Antonia quickly mopped the last bit of the aviary, filled the gull's food bowl with a mixture of bird seed and chopped fish, then carried the cleaning equipment outside.

"Watch it! I've already swept that bit—" Cai broke off in mid-sentence as his silver dolphin badge vibrated.

Antonia propped the mop up against the aviary. Her silver dolphin charm was fluttering against her neck and whistling loudly.

Silver Dolphin, we need you.

"Spirit, I hear your call," Antonia and Cai answered together.

At once they ran to the bottom of the garden and through the gate that led to the beach. The Sea Watch boat was pulled up on the sand and Antonia and Cai pulled off their trainers and socks and threw them inside. They raced for the sea, splashing through the water until it was too deep to run. Antonia dived into the water first, arching her body like a dolphin as she swam. Her legs melded

together like a tail and she kicked them joyfully. Being a Silver Dolphin was so wonderful. It made her forget the hurt she was feeling at Cai's unfriendly tone. Cai swam alongside her and side by side the Silver Dolphins raced to answer Spirit's call.

Chapter Four

They swam west, shadowing the coastline until a long while later Antonia saw Spirit, his magnificent silver head bobbing in the water as he waited for them.

"Thank you for answering my call, Silver Dolphins." Spirit rubbed noses with Antonia and Cai, then indicated that they should follow

him. He swam fast, occasionally checking the shore until at last he came to a tiny secluded beach. Spirit stopped suddenly and Antonia swerved to avoid crashing into his tail.

"That's strange," clicked Spirit. "A short while ago a porpoise was stranded in the surf. He seemed to be caught up in something."

Porpoises were small dolphin-like animals with blunt noses and little dorsal fins. They were shy creatures and neither Antonia nor Cai had seen one before.

"We'll check the beach," said Cai, even though he could see that it was empty.

They swam to the beach and paddled through the surf. Antonia pounced on a rotten coil of rope floating in the frothy water. It was slimy, with bits of seaweed hanging from it, and there was a dark stain in the middle.

"Yuk! That looks like blood," she said, holding it away from her.

"So where's the porpoise?" said Cai.

"Gone," said Antonia. "But it was definitely here. You can see the scuff marks it made in the sand. It must have somehow managed to free itself and swim away."

As the tide pulled back from the beach, Antonia pointed to a series of lines.

They stared at them until the sea came back and covered them again with frothy white surf.

"Lucky porpoise! It managed without us." Cai pushed his curly hair back from his face.

Antonia rolled the rope in her hands.

"Hmm," she said thoughtfully. "I think we should try and find it just in case it's badly hurt."

"That's a good point," said Cai.

Antonia rinsed the rope in the surf then tied

it round her waist so she could dispose of it safely later. Then they swam back to Spirit and he also agreed that the porpoise ought to be found.

"Bubbles, Dream and Star can help," he added, clicking for them to come.

Bubbles arrived so quickly that Antonia guessed he'd been hanging around waiting for them to finish their task. Dream and Star took a little longer to get there. Everyone split up, but after searching the area twice no one had found the porpoise.

"That's good," clicked Bubbles happily. "It means it can't have been that badly injured."

Antonia wanted to believe him, but a small part of her wasn't convinced.

"Can we play with the Silver Dolphins, Dad?" Bubbles asked.

Spirit smiled fondly. "Yes," he clicked. "Have fun."

"Bubbly! Let's play seaweed tag," clicked Bubbles excitedly. "I'm it. I know exactly where to find a piece of seaweed."

He dived under the water.

"Come on," clicked Dream, swimming in the opposite direction.

Cai followed, but Antonia hung back, her grey-green eyes searching the sea one last time. Finding nothing, she forced herself to stop worrying and hurried after Cai and Dream.

It was one of the maddest games of seaweed tag they'd ever played. Cai kept teasing Bubbles, letting him get a flipper's length away before sprinting off. Then he hid behind some rocks and jumped out at Bubbles as he swam past clicking, "You can't catch me."

Bubbles swam faster, tossing the seaweed about until finally he tagged Cai with it on the foot.

"You're it," he squeaked excitedly.

"Not for long," Cai replied, snatching the seaweed and chasing after Bubbles.

Antonia slowed, thinking she had time for a rest, but Cai turned suddenly and swam after her. He stretched out his arm to tag her with the seaweed and Antonia only just got away. She shot upwards, breaking through the water's surface then diving back down and swimming in the opposite direction. Bubbles had disappeared. Antonia swam round a pile of rocks expecting to find him hiding behind them, but found Dream instead.

"Sssh," clicked Dream. She waggled a flipper to show she wanted Antonia to join her.

Antonia crouched behind the rocks with Dream, trying hard not to giggle as Cai swam closer. They waited until the moment he came round the rocks then they quickly swam the other way.

"I see you!" exclaimed Cai, changing direction.

Antonia and Dream raced away with Cai in hot pursuit. He swiped the seaweed at Antonia, but she ducked and it landed on Dream.

"My turn," clicked Dream, immediately chasing after Cai.

Antonia swam the other way, looking for somewhere to hide. Two rocks leaning against each other looked promising. Antonia swam closer, jumping in surprise when a voice clicked, "Flipper Feet, in here."

"Where? I can't see you."

"Here!" Bubbles chuckled, peeping out from under the rocks. "Come and hide with me."

"Is there room?" whispered Antonia.

"Yes," said Bubbles, pulling his tail in.

Antonia squeezed in beside him and wrapped her arms round her so that nothing was sticking out. It was hard to keep still and impossible not to giggle. The sea vibrated as Cai swam closer. Antonia put a fist to her mouth, choking back the laughter as Cai swam straight past them.

"Let's chase after him," said Bubbles mischievously.

Quietly they swam from their hiding place and followed after Cai up to the surface. It wasn't long before he sensed their vibrations. He turned quickly, his brown eyes widening in surprise.

"Where did you come from?"

"Not telling," clicked Bubbles, splashing Cai with water.

Cai dropped the seaweed and splashed Bubbles back.

"Water fight!" clicked Bubbles happily.

"Girls against boys," called Dream, coming to join the fun.

The water fight finally ended when, gasping for breath, Antonia called for a truce. The dolphins basked in the water and Antonia floated on her back, making a star shape with her arms and legs as she stared up at the bright blue sky.

"This is my favourite place in the whole wide world," she said happily.

"Mine too," said Cai softly. "I love the sea. I can't ever imagine not living near it."

"Come and join our pod," clicked Bubbles. "Dad won't mind. Think of the fun we'd have."

Antonia pulled herself upright, pushing her wet hair from her face as she trod water.

"It would be fun, but what about our families? They'd miss us terribly and we'd miss them. But I never want to live anywhere else other than here. When I'm grown-up and I've got my own house, it's going to be in Sandy Bay, and it's going to have a sea view."

"Yeah. It's got to be by the sea," said Cai softly. He had a funny, far-away look in his eyes.

"Cai..." Antonia was about to ask him if everything was all right, but he talked over her.

"We'd better get back. There's a lot to do at Sea Watch and I'm only there until lunchtime. Mum and Dad are taking me out this afternoon."

"We'll come some of the way with you," clicked Dream.

"Bubbly," clicked Bubbles cheerfully. "Race you home. Last one back's a prawn."

"It won't be me!" shouted Cai, chasing after Bubbles.

"Nor me!" called Antonia as she sped after them.

Chapter Five

At lunchtime Cai went up to the house to eat with his mum and dad, so Antonia had her sandwiches on the beach with Emily, Karen, Eleanor and Oliver. Afterwards they skimmed stones, seeing who could make a stone bounce the most number of times across the sea's surface. Antonia was good at skimming and

got a stone to do four bounces, but Oliver was better and made his stone bounce five times.

They were searching for suitable pebbles when Claudia came down to find them.

"I've got to go and pick up a kittiwake with a fishing hook stuck in its leg. It's on the cliffs a mile or so from Crane Point. Does anyone want to come with me?"

"Me," said Antonia and Emily together.

"Great. Go and get in the car then. The lady who rang me is going to stay with the bird until we get there."

"Do you want me to get a bird carrier?" asked Antonia.

"Yes, please, and a pair of gloves," said Claudia. "I'll go and get my car keys. I left them indoors."

*   *   *

Claudia drove past Crane Point and after a while she pulled off the road and into a gravel car park. It was empty except for a blue car with its windows open and a brown Labrador sitting patiently in the boot.

"Here we are," said Claudia. "That must be the lady's car. She said her dog found the bird when they were on the way back from a cliff-top walk."

Taking the bird carrier and gloves from the boot, they walked past the car. A short distance away they saw a lady bending down to a grey and white bird. They hurried over and Claudia introduced everyone.

"Hello, I'm Claudia from Sea Watch, and this is Antonia and Emily."

"I'm Brenda. Thanks for coming so quickly," said the lady. "I haven't tried to take the

fishing hook out in case I made the injury worse."

The bird watched Claudia warily as she bent over it.

"Steady," she murmured. "We're not going to hurt you."

The kittiwake was a medium-sized bird with a yellow bill, a white head and underside and a grey back. Its black legs were tucked underneath it, but the bird shifted as Claudia approached, revealing a fishing hook stuck in the top of its leg. A length of thin nylon twine stretched around its leg and down to its webbed foot.

Claudia continued to murmur softly to the bird as she assessed its injury.

"That's nasty. I'm not going to try and remove the hook here either. We'll take the

bird back to Sea Watch. I might have to call the vet. Pass me the gloves, please, Emily. And bring the cage closer, Antonia. That's great. OK, open the door and stand back, everyone."

Antonia put the cage down and moved away. Emily went and stood beside her. With a deft movement, Claudia lifted the bird; it flinched, but never made a sound as she put it in the cage and closed the door.

Antonia and Emily waited patiently while Claudia explained to Brenda how they would treat the bird. Antonia was half listening when Emily made her jump by grabbing her arm and exclaiming, "A whale! Look, it's a whale."

"Where?" squeaked Antonia, spinning round.

"There," said Emily. "No, you're looking the wrong way. It's over there."

Antonia turned her head.

"Too late!" Emily sighed with disappointment. "It just dived under."

"Are you sure it was a whale?" asked Antonia, still scanning the sea. "I've never seen one round here. Could it have been a large dolphin?"

"It was a whale," insisted Emily. "I could tell from its fin. I wish I'd had my camera with me! That was amazing."

Brenda nodded excitedly.

"Whales are amazing. I saw one once when I was walking my dog Meg, but it wasn't round here. Which reminds me – I'd better get back. It's not fair to leave her in the car. It can get quite hot even at this time of the year."

She hurried off, but Antonia, Emily and Claudia remained where they were, staring

out at the sea, hoping for a glimpse of the whale.

"We better get this little chap home," said Claudia eventually.

Back at Sea Watch Claudia cut away the fishing twine and successfully removed the fishing hook from the bird's leg, but she decided to call the vet anyway.

"I should probably take the bird in for an antibiotic injection," she said.

Mr Singh told Claudia that he was coming her way and would call in at Sea Watch later.

"He's going to take a look at Rusty as well," said Claudia.

Antonia loved watching Mr Singh when he came to Sea Watch. He was an excellent vet, clearly explaining how he would treat each animal and patiently answering questions.

Antonia stayed at Sea Watch until the end of the day hoping to see him. Her last job was feeding Rusty. The little cub drank more than he had at lunchtime, but he still couldn't finish his bottle. Antonia recorded the amount on Rusty's chart then washed his bottle very slowly. Afterwards she took ages making up the sterilising solution to soak the bottle and teat in. Antonia was hovering around when Mr Singh rang to say he'd been delayed. Antonia was disappointed, but she couldn't wait any longer. Mum was strict about her being home on time and would ground her if she was late.

On the way home she bumped into Sophie.

"Hi there, what have you been up to?" asked Antonia, pleased to see her friend.

"Drawing," said Sophie, waving her sketch

book. "Guess what I saw? A dolphin! Look, I drew a picture of it."

Sophie opened her book and passed it to Antonia.

"That's really good, Soph," said Antonia admiringly. "But that's not a dolphin. The fin's the wrong shape. That looks more like a whale to me."

"A whale!" Sophie was astounded. "I didn't know we got whales round here."

"I've never seen one, but Emily did today when we were up on the cliffs."

"Wow!" said Sophie. "I've got to go and tell Dad. He's always wanted to paint whales. Bye, Antonia. Come round sometime."

"I will," Antonia called after her.

When Antonia got home she was restless and unable to settle. She decided to ring Cai

to find out what Mr Singh had said about Rusty and the kittiwake. She started to punch out the numbers on the key pad, then remembering what Mum had said about giving Cai space, slammed the receiver down. Antonia suddenly felt uncomfortable about interrupting Cai's time with his parents.

Jessica had gone to her friend Naomi's for tea and by the time she came home it was too late to play in the den. Antonia went to bed with a book, but she was too restless to concentrate on the story. She lay with the duvet pulled up to her nose and hoped that Cai would be at Sea Watch the next day.

Chapter Six

The following day there was good news. Mr Singh had given the kittiwake an antibiotic and its wound was recovering nicely. He was also pleased with Rusty's progress. He'd said that considering the cub was probably still in shock he was feeding quite well.

"It won't be long before he's draining that

bottle dry," he'd reassured Claudia. "Your biggest concern now is to socialise him with other foxes."

Cai was late starting at Sea Watch again. Antonia kept watching the door and her heart jumped when he finally arrived. She waved at him and, with a tight smile, he waved back. Antonia stared at Cai from under a curtain of hair. She was convinced that something was wrong. Her Cai was usually much bouncier than this new one. Claudia came over and asked if Antonia and Cai would take a supply of litter sacks down to the harbour for the fishermen. Recently they'd started bagging up the rubbish they caught in their fishing nets and disposing of it back at the harbour instead of tossing it into the sea.

On the way there Antonia chatted to Cai,

but he seemed distracted and answered her questions with single words and grunts. Sandy Bay was full of tourists and the pavements were crowded with slow-moving people.

"So many holiday-makers!" exclaimed Cai suddenly. He tutted crossly as he finally managed to overtake a family carrying a huge amount of beach things.

"They're good for the town," said Antonia mildly. "I just wish they'd take their litter home with them." She stooped to pick up an ice-lolly wrapper and Cai almost fell over her.

"Watch where you're going!" he exclaimed.

Antonia giggled and, giving him a friendly nudge, replied, "Watch where you're going yourself."

"Get off!" Cai shrugged her away.

Antonia was so surprised she stopped where

she was. Had her best friend really just shouted at her?

Cai kept walking, leaving Antonia staring after him in dismay. He didn't stop until he reached the harbour. Then he sat on a mooring buoy, moodily kicking it with his heels while waiting for Antonia to catch him up.

"We leave the sacks in the harbour-master's office, right?" he asked.

"Yes," said Antonia. Surely Cai wasn't still cross with her?

Cai weaved his way through the busy harbour to a small white building with a flower box full of brightly coloured primroses hanging under the window.

"That's pretty," said Antonia.

"Yeah, very pretty," said Cai, not sounding like he meant it.

When the harbour master opened the door, Cai was polite and friendly. He was totally different to how he'd been earlier. Antonia studied him out of the corner of her eye. Cai's behaviour was making her nervous. Antonia didn't want to admit it, but she had a sneaky feeling that she knew exactly what was wrong with Cai. She'd suspected it since yesterday, but didn't want to believe it was true. Now that Cai's parents were here in Sandy Bay he'd decided that he didn't want to live without them any more. Antonia didn't blame him, but she was shocked and upset that he hadn't shared this with her. They didn't keep secrets from each other. Unable to bear it any longer, she grabbed Cai's arm as he turned away from the harbour-master's office.

"We have to talk," she said firmly.

Cai went as stiff as a board, but at least he didn't shake Antonia off. He let her lead him to a private spot behind the harbour wall. Antonia sat down on a long wooden bench and after a moment's hesitation Cai sat beside her. He wouldn't look at her, though, and stared out to sea.

Antonia took a deep breath. "It's all right, I don't mind. Well I do, but I understand…"

Antonia knew she wasn't making any sense, so she started the conversation again.

"Look, Cai, I need to know the truth. Do you want to go and live with your parents in Australia?"

"No!" exploded Cai. His lip trembled and he bit it, closing his eyes as he fought back tears.

Antonia looked away, not wanting to upset him further.

"You've got it all wrong," Cai whispered at last. "Of course I miss Mum and Dad. I've been looking forward to their visit for ages. But I don't want to live in Australia. This is my home now, in Sandy Bay. I love living here with Aunty Claudia, and you and the dolphins, and all our friends. Mum and Dad work long hours. When we lived together I hardly ever saw them."

"So what's wrong then?" asked Antonia. "Why are you angry with me?"

"I'm not angry with you. I'm cross with my parents. They didn't plan on staying in Australia forever. At first it was for six months but then their contract was extended. Now they've been asked if they'd take permanent jobs there..." Cai's voice petered out.

"So what's the problem? Can't everything

just carry on as it was?" Antonia asked hesitantly.

"That's what I thought," said Cai, sighing heavily. "But Mum and Dad want us to be a proper family again. They've given me a choice: I can either move to Australia with them, or they'll go back to their old jobs... and we'll live in the city like we used to."

Antonia felt like someone had knocked all the breath out of her. She stared at Cai in disbelief.

"But..." Closing her eyes, she concentrated on breathing slowly and deeply, until her heart stopped racing. "So what are you going to do?"

"I don't know," said Cai tonelessly. "Aunty Claudia said I can stay with her whenever I like, but Mum and Dad said if we move to the city it would be too far to come back every

weekend. Visits would have to be kept for the holidays. And if we move to Australia I'd hardly ever get to visit…"

He fell silent and even though Antonia's mind was racing with questions, she didn't have enough breath to speak.

"I don't know what to do," Cai said miserably. "I'd rather stay in England so I can still see you and Aunty Claudia. But if that's only in the holidays, then how am I going to be a Silver Dolphin? At least if I move to Australia Mum and Dad have promised to buy a house near the beach. I wouldn't be able to help Spirit and his pod, but I'd get to be a Silver Dolphin all of the time."

"Can't your mum and dad move somewhere near the sea in England?" asked Antonia frantically.

Putting his head in his hands, Cai tugged at his dark, curly hair.

"I asked them that already," he muttered. "But the company they work for doesn't have an English office near the sea."

Antonia's heart was banging so hard the noise was hurting her ears. "So what are you going to do?" she asked.

"I don't know," said Cai defeatedly. "What should I do?"

Antonia didn't have an answer. She didn't want Cai to move to Australia because they might not see each other again. But the dolphins needed Cai too. How could he live in England if it meant only being a Silver Dolphin in the holidays?

"Checkmate," said Cai softly. "Whatever I do, I lose."

Chapter Seven

Antonia and Cai were very quiet for the rest of the day. Neither of them mentioned the decision facing Cai, but it was hanging over them like an enormous black question mark.

Late in the afternoon, as Antonia gave the little fox cub his milk, she was pleased to see he was more inquisitive and that he nearly finished a whole bottle of milk. Cai came in as Antonia was shutting the cub back into his pen.

"I'm going back to the house now. See you tomorrow. Don't forget Dad's taking us windsurfing in the morning."

"Can't wait," said Antonia, smiling even though she was hurting inside. She took longer than usual to check Rusty's cage and write up his notes. She was dreading going home, as she'd have to pretend to be cheerful.

The moment Antonia got back, Jessica wrapped her arms round her and refused to let her go until Antonia promised to play in her den after tea.

"I promise!" squeaked Antonia, wriggling free.

Playing with Jessica was fun and Antonia managed not to worry about Cai for a while. But alone in bed in the dark the problem niggled away at her, making her tummy ache. Sleep was impossible. Antonia distracted herself by reading until Mum came up and told her to switch off the light. Then Antonia tossed and turned – hot, thirsty and uncomfortable – until the small hours when, finally exhausted, she fell asleep.

The following morning her eyes were gritty with tiredness, but Antonia got up when her alarm went off and had breakfast with Mum and Dad.

"You're up early again," said Dad.

"I'm going windsurfing with Cai – we're meeting at Sea Watch," Antonia explained.

Dad ran her to Sea Watch in his car before starting work at his garage. Cai was already there feeding Rusty. Antonia went to help, tidying Rusty's pen and refreshing his water dish.

"We haven't got long," said Cai, as he carefully put Rusty back. "Dad booked us an early lesson."

Luckily lots of volunteers arrived as Claudia was sharing out the jobs. Emily, Karen and Eleanor offered to clean out the birds, so Antonia and Cai volunteered to quickly mop down the area around the deepwater pool.

"This will have to be our last job," said Cai, checking his watch.

They were halfway round the pool when a familiar tingling sensation came over Antonia.

She stopped mopping, pushing her long, blonde hair back over her shoulder as she stood up straight.

"Oi!" called Cai good-naturedly. "Stop skiving."

"I'm not," said Antonia, as her silver dolphin charm thrummed against her neck.

Cai's charm started vibrating too, its tiny tail flicking rhythmically against his neck.

Silver Dolphin, we need you.

Spirit's voice rang out in the air and inside Antonia's head.

Spirit, I'm on my way, Antonia silently answered him back.

"Spirit, I'm coming," called Cai.

But it was almost time to go windsurfing. It wouldn't be fair on Cai's dad if they both missed the lesson.

"I'll answer the call," said Antonia decisively. "Go windsurfing with your dad."

"No way!" said Cai emphatically. "I'm a Silver Dolphin. I'm answering the call too."

"What about the lesson?"

"We'll worry about that later," said Cai. "Come on. It might be urgent."

They abandoned their mops, locking the gate behind them as they exited the pool. Shoulder to shoulder, Antonia and Cai ran to the bottom of the garden and squeezed through the gate on to the beach. They stopped to pull their trainers and socks off then threw them inside the Sea Watch boat before running into the sea. A light breeze ruffled the waves as they waded deeper until finally it was safe to dive in.

Antonia surged ahead, hands pushing

against the water like flippers, kicking her legs like a dolphin's tail as they melded together. Cai swam alongside her and they synchronised their strokes; rising from the sea, their bodies gracefully arched in time as they leapt the waves and dived back into the water.

Antonia sighed with pleasure. She loved this moment best of all. Becoming a Silver Dolphin was so thrilling and she knew it always would be. *But what if she had to give it up?* A sharp pain seared through her as she thought about Cai and the decision he faced. Antonia's pace faltered and Cai began to pull ahead. Pushing away these unwelcome thoughts, Antonia concentrated on being a Silver Dolphin. She swam westward, letting Spirit's vibrations guide her until she saw his silver body in the distance.

As Antonia and Cai drew closer, Spirit called out to them. "Hurry, I've found the porpoise and he's badly injured."

When they were a dolphin-length away, Spirit dived under the water, flicking his tail for them to follow him. They swam down, passing a school of fish, a coral bed and a garden of seaweed. There were lots of rocks on the seabed and Spirit slowed, weaving his way between them as he searched for the porpoise.

"He's here," he clicked at last.

A large crab was tucked under the base of the rocks and it waved a threatening claw as Spirit approached. Spirit kept his distance as he swam round it and Antonia and Cai followed his example. The first part Antonia saw of the porpoise was its blunt nose just

visible behind a rock. She approached slowly, making reassuring clicking noises. The porpoise tensed as if he might suddenly swim away.

"It's OK, we're here to help," clicked Antonia.

Spirit fell back, letting Antonia and Cai slowly edge towards the frightened creature. Soon they were close enough to see a torn flipper hanging uselessly from the porpoise's side. It took a lot of control not to rush forward, but Antonia moved slowly knowing that a sudden movement might scare the porpoise away. At last she was in touching distance. She trod water while waiting for a sign that the porpoise was ready to trust her. The porpoise looked straight at her, its dark eyes pleading. Antonia stretched out and lightly

stroked the creature along his black and white cheek.

"I can't promise to make you better," she whispered, "but I'll do my best."

Chapter Eight

Slowly, the porpoise relaxed. Antonia moved closer, running her hand along its body until she reached the damaged flipper, crusty with old blood.

"Steady," she whispered, laying both hands on it. "I'm going to help you."

Firmly but gently, Antonia manipulated the

flipper until the torn bits matched up. Holding it together with one hand she ran her other hand along the join, pressing firmly on it.

Heal.

A warm feeling rushed along her arms and into her fingers.

Heal.

Her fingers tingled as the warmth spread through them. Antonia kept pressing on the wound, willing it to heal. After a bit she was dimly aware of movement to the side of her. A second porpoise was hesitantly coasting in the water a tail's length away. Antonia was glad. It was good to have friends, especially when you were hurt. The damaged flipper wasn't difficult to mend, but it took time and a lot of concentration. At last the tingling sensation in Antonia's fingers began to

weaken. She held her breath as she pulled her hands away to examine the flipper. There wasn't much to see, just a faint scar line. Experimentally, the porpoise moved the flipper. Amazingly it seemed fine. He stared at Antonia as if he was saying thank you, then seconds later he and his friend swam away.

"Well done, Silver Dolphin," clicked Spirit.

"That was brilliant. I'll never get over how you can heal animals," agreed Cai.

They swam to the surface together. Then Spirit said goodbye, rubbing his nose against theirs and ruffling Antonia's hair with his flipper. Even though they were in a hurry to get back, Antonia and Cai watched Spirit swim away.

"You know," said Cai suddenly, "you didn't

need me here today. You could have managed on your own."

"I thought you wanted to come," said Antonia.

"I did. But what I meant was you're a very powerful Silver Dolphin. If… if I go away you'll manage fine without me."

"It won't be the same," said Antonia in a small voice. She felt sick inside. Had Cai reached a decision already? Antonia wasn't sure that she was ready to hear it.

"Nothing's going to be the same," said Cai, sighing heavily. "Come on. We'd better go or we'll be late for our windsurfing lesson."

They swam back to Claudia's beach in silence. Cai was out of the water first and bounded up the sand, sea water draining off him as he ran. At the Sea Watch boat he

stopped and pulled Antonia's shoes out, handing them to her when she caught him up.

"Thanks. That was good timing. There's your dad," said Antonia, spotting Mr Pacific at the gate.

"I've found you at last!" called Mr Pacific, sounding relieved. "Did you forget the time? Hurry up or we're going to be late."

"Sorry, Dad," Cai apologised. "We had an important job to do for Sea Watch."

"Now there's a surprise! Sea Watch! It's all you ever talk about," said Mr Pacific.

The windsurfing school was a twenty-minute drive from Sandy Bay. Mr Pacific chivvied everyone into Claudia's car, including his wife, who was carrying a video camera to film the lesson. It took Cai's dad a while to get used

to both the car and the narrow country lanes and he drove slowly, arriving at the windsurfing school with only a few minutes to spare. Hurriedly, Antonia and Cai wriggled into their wetsuits while Mr Pacific checked them in and hired a wetsuit for himself.

"Sure you won't join us?" Cai asked his mum.

"Uh-uh," said Mrs Pacific, shaking her head. "Someone's got to work the camera."

Antonia giggled. "You sound like my mum," she said.

The windsurfing lesson was great fun. First, there was a session on the beach on how to get started. They learnt how to put the sail together, get the board into the water and the correct way to stand on it. Antonia and Cai listened carefully, eager to get it right and

make the most of their time on the water. At last the land part of the lesson was over and they were allowed to take their windsurfing boards into the sea.

"It's not as easy as surfing," Antonia called to Cai, as she tried to raise her sail from the water having accidentally dropped it for the umpteenth time.

"I keep losing the wind," Cai shouted back. His sail hung limply and he shifted his weight on the board, desperately trying to fill the sail with wind. The board turned, but Cai didn't get the angle right. The sail flapped feebly then the windsurfing mast tipped over, almost throwing Cai into the water.

"Rats!" he exclaimed, shifting his feet and pulling hard on the rig to raise the sail from the sea.

"I'm up again," shouted Antonia, who had also dropped her sail. "Come on, Cai, you can do it."

Mr Pacific was surprisingly good at windsurfing and when the lesson was over he confessed that he'd done it a few times in Australia.

"If we decide to live there then I'm going to get a windsurfing board. You can have one too, Cai."

"I prefer surfing, thanks," said Cai woodenly.

"The surfing's great in Australia," said Mr Pacific enthusiastically. "The breakers are unbelievable and the sea's much warmer than it is here."

"Wimp!" said Cai rudely.

"Cai," Mrs Pacific warned him.

It was embarrassing hearing Cai being rude

to his parents. Antonia concentrated on peeling off her wetsuit, pretending that she hadn't heard him.

Mr Pacific shrugged. "He's right. I am a wimp. I don't like the cold. It must be my West Indian blood. What I need now is a hot drink and something to eat. The beach shop is doing cream teas. How about you go and grab a table and I'll get us all a cream tea?"

"Sounds lovely," said Mrs Pacific. "Cai and Antonia can find a table. I'll come and help you."

Antonia and Cai picked an outside table close to the beach and plonked themselves down on the plastic chairs surrounding it.

"Sounds like your dad's really keen on Australia," said Antonia, her voice wavering a bit.

Cai grunted something back. Antonia gazed around, not sure what to say next. She'd never been at a loss for words with Cai before. She didn't like the awkward feeling that was suddenly there between them. A torn plastic bag lay half buried in the sand. Glad for an excuse to move, Antonia went and picked it up.

"Wait for me," said Cai, jumping on to the sand and running after her.

Stooping down, he picked up a half-crushed drinks can and held it out to put in the carrier bag.

Cai grinned. "We make a good team."

"The best," Antonia replied, grinning back.

By the time Mr and Mrs Pacific came out of the beach shop, each carrying a tray loaded

with teapots, mugs, plates of warm scones, clotted cream and jam, Antonia and Cai had half filled the bag with rubbish.

Mrs Pacific was impressed to see them litter-picking on the beach. "You're not at Sea Watch now," she teased.

"Sea Watch isn't just a place," said Cai. "The things we do at Sea Watch matter wherever we are. Over a million seabirds die every year from litter-related injuries, and that's just birds! Animals like turtles, dolphins and porpoises all die too."

Mrs Pacific stared at Cai for a moment. "That's a lot of animals," she said eventually.

"It's one million too many," said Cai.

Antonia put the bag of rubbish in the bin, then she and Cai went inside the beach shop to wash their hands. They were starving after

such a busy morning and piled their scones high with jam and cream.

"That was delicious," said Mr Pacific only a few minutes later, pushing his empty plate away. "I could eat it all again."

"If we stay in Sandy Bay, you could have a cream tea every day," said Cai pointedly.

"I could," said Mr Pacific, then he rather abruptly changed the subject by asking if anyone wanted a walk before they went back to Sandy Bay.

They set off along the beach and round the headland. The tide was slowly going out and Antonia and Cai took off their shoes so they could paddle in the sea. Cai was silent again and Antonia could guess what he was thinking. Her stomach churned queasily and she wished she hadn't eaten so much.

Antonia desperately wanted Cai to stay in England so she could still see him in the holidays. But she knew she was being unfair. Cai ought to move to Australia where he could be a Silver Dolphin all the time. Antonia wanted to tell Cai this, but the words got stuck in her throat. Hating herself for being cowardly, she picked up a pebble and hurled it into the sea.

Chapter Nine

There was a small green van parked on Claudia's driveway when they got home so Mr Pacific left the car in the road.

"Let's go see who it is," said Cai.

"Maybe it's a delivery driver bringing the supplies Claudia ordered," said Antonia.

"That's good. We're nearly out of

disposable gloves. Let's go and help unpack."

"Honestly!" exclaimed Mrs Pacific, shaking her head. "You both live and breathe Sea Watch."

Cai slowed and called over his shoulder, "You can come too. Helping out at Sea Watch is great fun."

"I'm sure it is, but I'll give it a miss today," said Mrs Pacific. She shivered and pulled her jacket round her. "I'm going indoors. I'm still not used to this chilly spring weather."

"This isn't chilly!" Cai shouted back.

He darted off again with Antonia hot on his heels. On the way down the garden they nearly collided with Claudia and a woman carrying a cage, walking the other way.

"You're back!" Claudia said, sounding

relieved. "This is Jackie from the Sandy Bay Badger Sanctuary; remember her? She's taking Rusty now. I thought you were going to miss saying goodbye."

Antonia's heart sank and without meaning to she blurted out, "Does Rusty have to go?"

"It's the best thing for him," said Jackie gently. "Foxes are social animals. We have other cubs at the sanctuary. Rusty can play with them and learn the skills he'll need when we release him back into the wild."

"Yes, of course," Antonia felt silly and wished she hadn't said anything.

"This has happened faster than we thought," said Claudia sympathetically. "But it's great that the sanctuary has room for Rusty."

"We put news of our animals on our

website," said Jackie. "And you can ring us at any time for a progress report. You've got my number."

"Thanks, we'll do that," said Claudia.

"Bye, Rusty." Antonia gave him a long look to remember him by.

"Bye, Rusty," echoed Cai.

The little cub pressed his nose up to the bars, but Antonia and Cai didn't move. They knew they mustn't treat him like a pet. They followed Jackie to her van and watched as she loaded the cage into the back and shut the doors.

"That's it then," said Cai as the van pulled away.

Antonia nodded because she couldn't trust herself to speak. Tears were welling up in her eyes, but not for Rusty – her tears were for

Cai. How soon before the goodbyes were for him? Claudia was very quiet too and suddenly Antonia realised that his great-aunty would miss Cai as much as she would.

It's not fair, she thought.

Sometimes life isn't, so you make the best of it, Claudia silently answered her.

On impulse, Claudia reached out and gave Antonia then Cai a quick hug.

"What was that for?" squeaked Cai indignantly.

"Just because!" said Claudia with a smile. "Right, there's a fox pen to be cleaned out. Would you two like to do it or have you got other plans?"

"We'll do it," said Antonia and Cai together.

They cleaned the fox pen thoroughly and when it was done they swept and mopped

the floor of the back room. Then the supplies Claudia was waiting for arrived and Antonia and Cai helped to carry them from the back of the van to the Sea Watch building. The delivery driver was delighted.

"If all my runs are this easy I'll finish early today," he said.

Antonia and Cai helped unpack and put everything away, then Claudia gave them crisps, apples and a jug of fruit juice.

"Let's take this outside. We could sit on the beach," said Cai.

They carefully carried their snacks down on to the sand. They sat with their backs resting against the stern of the Sea Watch boat so they could look out to sea. Cai finished his apple and began digging a hole in the sand. Deeper and deeper he dug until

Antonia asked, "What are you building?"

"A tunnel to the other side of the world," said Cai. "So you can visit me in Australia."

Antonia's face flushed and her heart began to thud loudly.

"You're going then?"

Cai dug faster, piling the sand up at the edge of his deepening hole.

"I don't know, Antonia. I *can't* go back to my old city life. Not now I know I'm a Silver Dolphin. I need to live by the sea. But that means moving to Australia and hardly ever seeing you, so I don't want that either."

He scooped up a handful of sand and let it trickle through his fingers.

"Time's running out. Mum and Dad have to let work know what they want to do. If I don't decide soon then they'll make the

decision for me. I begged them to look for new jobs here in Sandy Bay, but they both said it wasn't an option."

Antonia's hands trembled as she prepared herself to speak.

"Go to Australia—" Her voice cracked and she cleared her throat before continuing. "You know you have to. Being a Silver Dolphin is much more important than anything. The work we do saves lives!"

They sat in silence. Cai continued to scoop up the sand and run it through his fingers. Antonia concentrated on her breathing, forcing herself not to cry.

"I'll tell Mum and Dad tonight then." Cai's voice was barely a whisper. "I don't want to, but you're right – being a Silver Dolphin is more important than anything."

"We can email," said Antonia bravely.

"And there's Skype," said Cai. "You know, where you use your computer to talk to people. You can see them and everything. I Skype with Mum and Dad all the time. Once you've got a webcam, all the calls are free."

"I'll have to ask Mum and Dad if we can get it straight away."

Antonia put her half-finished apple down. She couldn't eat any more.

"When do you think you'll go?" she asked.

"Mum and Dad wanted me to go back with them. It's all right, though," he added quickly. "They realised that wasn't such a good idea. They've got to find me a school place and they can't apply for that until we know where we're going to live. Aunty Claudia suggested that I stay with her until the beginning of the

summer holidays. So we've got a whole term left."

Term time usually dragged on forever, but Antonia had a feeling that this next one would rush by.

"I'm going to miss you," she whispered. "But I'm so glad you still get to be a Silver Dolphin."

"Me too," said Cai.

Chapter Ten

Once Cai had made his decision to go to Australia, Antonia developed a gnawing ache in her stomach that wouldn't go away. She put on a show of cheerfulness at Sea Watch, but at home she moped around with a face as long as the River Nile.

Mum and Dad were sympathetic to start

with, but they soon lost patience with her.

"Stop dwelling on the future, which you can't change, and enjoy the time you have left with Cai," said Mum briskly.

It was good advice and Antonia did her best to be cheerful, but inside she still felt totally miserable. She knew Cai did too. He'd lost his spark and Antonia grew angry with Mr and Mrs Pacific, blaming them for stealing the real Cai from her. She avoided them as much as she could, which wasn't that difficult as they rarely came to Sea Watch. Then one day Cai asked Antonia to visit the local aquarium with him and his parents.

"You will come, won't you?" he asked eagerly. "We're going to visit Legs. Claudia told Mum and Dad about the rescue and they want to go and see him."

Legs was an octopus that Antonia and Cai had saved from an abandoned fishing pot. Antonia was keen to visit Legs in his new home at the aquarium, but wasn't sure if she wanted to go with Mr and Mrs Pacific. But she couldn't refuse Cai, so she went. Cai's parents were as nice as they always were and in the end Antonia had a great time. Will and Tim, two of the aquarium staff who'd helped rescue Legs, gave them a special VIP's tour of the aquarium, including the staff-only places.

"What's going to happen to Legs?" asked Cai, staring at the octopus, who was in a tank of his own.

"He's going home! We're releasing him back into the Mediterranean Sea," said Tim.

"When?" asked Cai.

"When we've stopped arguing about who's going to fly to Spain with him," joked Will.

"That was such fun," said Mrs Pacific as they walked from the aquarium back to the car. "Is there anywhere else you'd like to go before your dad and I fly home? Antonia can come too, of course."

"Not really," Cai sighed. "I'd rather spend the time at Sea Watch. Why don't you come and help too? You'd love it."

"Thanks, but this is supposed to be a holiday. We'll leave the hard work to you two," said Mrs Pacific.

Cai threw himself into Sea Watch, arriving first and staying until Claudia closed up for the night. When there were only three days before his mum and dad were due to fly back to Australia, Claudia suggested that he

should spend the remaining time with his parents.

"Why?" asked Cai. "I'll be spending every day with them soon."

"That's three months away," said Claudia quietly, but she didn't mention the subject again.

Later that afternoon, Antonia and Cai were tidying up at Sea Watch when a very familiar sensation swept over Antonia. Her stomach bubbled with anticipation and she glanced at Claudia. She gave her a meaningful look back. Antonia quickly dumped the things she'd been carrying on a nearby shelf and wiped her dusty hands down her trousers.

"That's tidy?" asked Cai, raising his eyebrows.

"I'll do it properly later," said Antonia, eyeing the door.

Right then Antonia felt her silver dolphin charm vibrate against her neck. Cai jumped, his hand flying to cover his own charm as Spirit's whistling cry shrilled round the room.

Cai grinned apologetically. "Sorry, Aunty Claudia, but you're going to have to manage without us."

"No problem," she calmly answered.

Antonia and Cai raced out of Sea Watch and down the garden, jumping over the gate to the beach for speed.

"I wonder what Spirit wants," Cai panted as he ran. "It must be important the way my charm's vibrating."

"Mine too," said Antonia. Her charm was thrashing around as if life depended on it.

Antonia hopped along the beach, pulling her shoes and socks off as she went and tossing them into the Sea Watch boat. She hurried into the sea, wading deeper until the water came up to her thighs and then she threw herself into the sea. It was cold and the shock of it made her gasp out loud, but she quickly recovered as her legs melded together like a dolphin tail. Squeaking with delight, Antonia propelled herself forward; arching her back and leaping in and out of the sea, she swam faster than a real dolphin to answer Spirit's call.

Cai swam alongside her and they urged each other on with little clicking noises. It was exhilarating racing through the sea together and for the first time in days Antonia forgot about the aching feeling in her stomach. They swam for ages, keeping up the same manic pace, until Antonia noticed a small yacht in the distance.

"We'll have to dive or someone might see us," she clicked to Cai.

They dipped under the water and swam down until they were a meter above the seabed. Before long they could see the boat's hull above them, covered in barnacles and bits of seaweed.

Suddenly, Cai exclaimed, "Careful! There's another boat over there."

"Two," Antonia corrected him. "Strange, there's not normally this amount of traffic in the water."

"Maybe it's a race," Cai suggested.

"Can't be, or all the boats would be the same type," said Antonia thoughtfully.

"They're all going the same way as us," said Cai.

"Are you sure?" Antonia hoped that Cai was

mistaken. It was tricky enough keeping out of one boat's way, but avoiding several would be far more difficult. What if the risk of being seen was too great to answer Spirit's call? Anxiously, Antonia swam on, but each time she looked back she could see the hulls of the boats following them. It made her very uncomfortable. Was it just a coincidence that they were travelling the same way as the Silver Dolphins? Antonia swam faster, anxious to reach Spirit. A short while later she sensed his vibrations in the water.

Relieved, she called to Cai, "We're nearly there."

"We've swum for miles!" exclaimed Cai, looking around. "See that estuary mouth over there? I think that's where the River Tam joins the sea."

"Is it?" said Antonia in surprise. "We did come miles. And look, there's Spirit."

There were several more boats near the estuary mouth. Antonia was concentrating on avoiding their rudders and propellers so at first she didn't notice that Spirit was accompanied by Star, Bubbles, Dream and several other dolphins from his pod. Her delight was quickly quelled by the serious expressions on all their faces. Even Bubbles had a worried look in his dark eyes. Antonia and Cai trod water as Spirit greeted them with a brief nose rub.

"Thank you for answering my call," he clicked. "This is urgent."

Chapter Eleven

"What's happened?" Antonia asked.

"A whale keeps trying to swim up the river. We've tried to guide her back out to sea, but she won't go. We need your help before she gets stuck or grounds herself."

"A whale!" exclaimed Antonia, nervously

glancing behind her. Whales were enormous creatures and she wasn't sure she wanted to get too close to one.

"Wicked!" whistled Cai, his voice low.

"She's very determined," Spirit continued. "Three times we've turned her back. She keeps giving us the slip, though. See those boats over there? The people on board have realised that the whale is in danger if she heads upstream. See how they've started to try to block the river's mouth?"

Antonia remained silent, remembering when they'd helped some dolphins who were beached in a smaller estuary. It had been awful – one of the dolphins had died. Unfortunately, those dolphins were already stranded by the time they'd gone to help them. Hopefully this should be easier, as long as the whale didn't get angry or attack anyone. Suddenly, she wrinkled her nose.

"Pooh, what's that awful smell?"

"What smell?" asked Cai.

"*That* smell!" exclaimed Antonia. "It's like rotting fish."

"Gross!" gagged Cai, getting a whiff of it. "That's disgusting. It's reminds me of... hang on, I know what that is! It's the whale. It must be a minke – Aunty Claudia said their breath stinks."

As the smell grew stronger, Antonia felt vibrations in the water and nervously moved closer to Cai.

"It's all right," he whispered reassuringly. "They only eat plankton and fish."

The vibrations continued until suddenly a torpedo-like shape shot past. Antonia stared

at it in awe. The minke whale was eight metres long and had a sharp nose and a pointed head with two blowholes. She had a black back and white underside with smoky grey patches where the two colours met. She was amazingly agile, zipping round the dolphins and boats with the grace of a dancer.

"Wow!" said Cai.

"Quick," said Antonia, "she's heading straight for the river's mouth."

They chased after her with Spirit and his pod in pursuit and as they caught her up Cai called out, "Split up to head her off."

Keeping underwater, he swam to the right and Antonia went to the left. She overtook the minke whale and raced towards the mouth of the river. There were many boats and Antonia forgot her worries about the minke as she

concentrated on avoiding their hulls. It was quite dangerous as a couple of the boats had seen the whale and were also moving to intercept it. Antonia had one heart-stopping moment when she almost swam straight into the hull of a cruiser. Turning a somersault, she missed the boat by millimetres.

Trembling from shock she slowed down, but there wasn't time for a long recovery. The whale was zipping around, appearing where she was least expected. Antonia sped on and overtook her at the mouth of the estuary. Bravely, Antonia joined forces with Cai, Spirit and the other dolphins. Swimming in a long line they barred the way into the river. Without hesitation the minke whale swam at the barricade. Antonia was scared, but she held her ground as the whale came closer. Then

at the last minute the minke grunted and veered away.

"Phew!" said Cai, grinning at Antonia.

But it wasn't over. Turning in a wide circle the whale came back, heading straight for Bubbles, the smallest dolphin in the barricade. Brave Bubbles barely flinched and once again the whale was forced to turn back. Time and again she returned, swimming at the dolphins, leaving it to the last possible moment before veering away. Refusing to be intimidated, they stood their ground, blocking the river mouth until finally the whale sped angrily away.

"She'll be back," said Spirit with certainty.

There was nothing to do but to keep a lookout for the whale's return. The dolphins relaxed, drifting in the water, sometimes surfacing for air. Cautiously, Antonia and Cai

each took a turn at surfacing and they were stunned by the increased number of boats sailing towards the mouth of the river estuary.

"What's going on?" asked Cai.

"It looks like someone radioed for help," said Antonia.

Suddenly, a picture of Claudia came into her head and then she heard her friend's voice speaking to her.

Are you with the whale?

Yes. How did you know?

Jack the coastguard rang. He's calling on local boat owners to come and help. Be careful, Silver Dolphin. There are lots of boats on their way. I'm sailing with some of them.

We'll be very careful, promised Antonia.

"Claudia's on her way here," she said to

Cai, who knew they could read each other's minds.

"Good," he replied. "We're going to need all the help we can get."

They drifted around on the seabed with Bubbles and Dream. Bubbles grew restless and swam in circles, turning speedy somersaults to change direction. Antonia began to wonder if everyone was mistaken. The whale wasn't coming back, was she? She was about to suggest they swim out to sea to look for her when she sensed something in the water heading towards them at speed.

"It's her," shouted Cai.

Antonia tensed as everyone immediately took up their positions across the river's mouth. What would happen if the whale didn't stop? But this time, with so many

boats in her way, it was much easier to force the minke to turn back. The whale grew more distressed as she tried to find a way through to the river. Despite her size she was so quick it was impossible to track her movements. She seemed to be everywhere. Her attempt lasted much longer this time and Antonia hated seeing her distress. The whale fought a long, hard battle to enter the river before she finally gave up. Dispirited, she swam away, her black and white body dappled in the sun-spangled water.

Plucking a strand of seaweed from the seabed, Antonia thoughtfully wound it round her finger. Something wasn't right. Why did the whale keep trying to return? She continued winding the seaweed in a fat,

green band round her finger until there was nothing left. Then, as she slowly unwound it, the answer came to her.

Turning to Cai, she asked breathlessly, "Why did Spirit call us?"

Cai stared at her in surprise. "We're the Silver Dolphins."

"No!" Antonia almost shouted with excitement. "Silver Dolphins can only help an animal if the problem has been caused by pollution or humans. So why did Spirit call us? I can't see anything that's causing the whale to swim up the river. It's her choice."

Cai's eyes widened. "You're right," he said. "We're missing something, aren't we?"

"Yes!" said Antonia triumphantly. "Before we can help the whale we need to find out what the real problem is."

Antonia's brain felt like it was lost in the middle of a fog. She glanced around, hoping for inspiration, but none came.

"Let's swim up the river," suggested Cai. "It's where the whale is trying to go, so maybe we'll find the answer there."

Chapter Twelve

he Silver Dolphins told Spirit their plan. "Good luck," he clicked, ruffling their hair with a flipper.

Antonia led the way, her tummy almost touching the sand as she swam under a small motorboat to get into the river. She stayed underwater until she was sure she was far

enough away from the boats not to be noticed. Then pointing upwards to tell Cai where she was going, she surfaced. He came up alongside her and they paddled in the water for a minute, taking deep breaths of the fresh spring air.

"Ready to go on?" asked Cai.

Antonia nodded and they swam alongside each other, Antonia looking to her left and Cai to his right. It was very peaceful after all the activity at the mouth of the estuary. The river was surrounded by woods on one side and a lush green meadow on the other. Hidden in the trees, birds chirped out their songs and a few noisy seagulls mewed overhead.

"There's nothing here," said Cai.

"I thought there might be buildings," said Antonia. "I was expecting a burglar alarm

ringing or something. Whales hear by sonar and can get confused by things like that."

"Maybe," said Cai. "Let's see if there are any buildings further down."

In silence they swam on, but the river scenery was totally unspoilt by any kind of development.

"There's nothing," said Cai finally. "Shall we go back?"

"Let's just go to the bend," Antonia suggested, not willing to admit defeat.

They swam on until they reached the bend. Antonia stopped and trod water, sighing with disappointment.

"There must be something else," she said. "Think! What are we missing?"

Cai didn't answer and Antonia realised he was swimming on.

"Cai," she called. "Let's go back."

"Hang on," said Cai, swimming towards the bank. "I just want to look on the other side of that tree. I thought I saw... Antonia, quick! You'll never guess what."

Cai's voice rose with excitement as he swam towards a large willow tree gracefully trailing its branches in the water.

"What is it?" asked Antonia. Burning with curiosity, she raced after Cai. "Oh my goodness, no wonder the whale was so frantic."

Pressed against the river bank, half concealed by the willow tree, was a female minke whale calf. Antonia couldn't take her eyes off the calf as she swam towards it.

"What's she doing up here?"

"She must have somehow got separated

from her mum and lost her way," said Cai, slowing to let Antonia catch up. "Maybe she followed a boat. It happens."

As they approached, the calf shifted, sending waves of water over the bank. Sensing her distress, Antonia stopped and motioned for Cai to do the same. The water was shallow enough to stand in. They stood quietly until the calf began to relax. But each time they took a step nearer she became agitated and thrashed around in the water.

"Steady," Antonia murmured. "We won't hurt you."

Very slowly, Antonia and Cai edged closer. The calf eyed them suspiciously, but gradually she relaxed. At last they were close enough to inspect her.

"See that small gash above her tail?" said

Antonia. "It looks like she caught herself on a boat's propeller. I think you're right – she must have followed a boat."

"She's had a lucky escape!" whistled Cai. "That injury could have been much worse."

Slowly reaching out, Antonia ran her hand along the young whale's soft, warm body until her fingers were resting on the gash. It would probably heal on its own, but Antonia didn't want to leave anything to chance.

Heal, she thought, concentrating on repairing the wound.

A warm tingling feeling rushed down her arm and into her fingers, then just as quickly it faded away. Antonia lifted her hand and saw that the wound had healed completely.

"Time to get this little one back to her mum," she said.

It was easier said than done. The whale wasn't stuck, but she was lost and disorientated. At first Antonia and Cai tried to encourage her back up the river by getting between her and the bank and herding her out. The calf eyed them warily and refused to move, so Antonia waded deeper, encouraging her with clicking noises. Still the whale didn't budge, but she flapped her tail in distress.

"We'll have to push her," said Cai eventually.

They stood on either side of the calf and pushed her into the river. She was too bewildered to struggle, but once they let her go she turned and swam quickly in the other direction.

"Oh no!" groaned Antonia, chasing after her.

"Quick!" panted Cai. "We need to turn her. The river's getting narrower and she'll get stuck if she goes any further."

They overtook the calf and swam in front of her. The calf hesitated then tried to swim round them. Antonia and Cai stretched out their arms and forced her back. Thankfully the calf wasn't as determined as her mother and, finally admitting defeat, she turned around.

"Hooray!" cheered Cai.

"It's not over yet," said Antonia. "Come on, before she changes her mind."

The calf swam underwater with her sickle-shaped fin sticking above the surface. Antonia and Cai swam on either side of her and as they neared the estuary's mouth the calf suddenly accelerated away.

"Do you think she can sense her mother?" called Cai.

Antonia was about to agree when her heart skipped a beat. *How could they have been so stupid?* The calf wouldn't be able to swim out into the open sea because of all the boats stopping her mother from swimming the other way. There was no time to lose. They had to get the barricade shifted before the calf reached it.

Chapter Thirteen

At first Antonia's mind filled with crazy visions of her and Cai racing ahead of the calf to warn the boat owners to move. But it would take too much explaining – they couldn't risk exposing the Silver Dolphins' secret. Antonia's brain whirled as it searched for another solution. Then all at once she had it. *Claudia!*

She could get the boats to move while Spirit stopped the mother whale from slipping through the gap.

Claudia.

Antonia imagined Claudia's face framed by her curly, windswept hair and her sea-green eyes.

Silver Dolphin, what's up?

Antonia sighed with relief.

We swam up the estuary. We found a minke whale calf. She's coming your way. Can you get the boats to move?

No problem.

Antonia grinned triumphantly. You could rely on Claudia to get things done without making others ask too many questions.

"What are you looking so smug about?" called Cai.

"Claudia's getting the boats to move," said Antonia.

"Well done! I'd never have thought of that!" Cai confessed.

They were nearly at the mouth of the estuary. Ahead, Antonia could see a group of boats in the water and to her delight some of them were already moving out to sea.

"Keep out of sight," she called to Cai.

The whale calf suddenly began swimming even faster. Antonia and Cai dived underwater where they wouldn't be seen and followed her.

"She won't turn back now," said Cai confidently.

"Let's hope so," said Antonia cautiously, not wanting to tempt fate.

There were so many boats in the water,

Antonia and Cai nearly missed the minke calf being reunited with her mother. They were swimming underwater round, the hull of a small fishing vessel when the mother whale appeared from nowhere and descended on her calf. She swam joyfully round, nudging her baby with her nose as if she couldn't quite believe she was real. The calf swam closer to its mum, nestling against her side, and then they headed out to sea.

"Well done, Silver Dolphins," said Spirit, swimming up with Star, Bubbles and Dream. "That was excellent work."

Bubbles came forward and high-fived Antonia and Cai with his tail. Dream did the same and Star nuzzled them with her nose.

"It's not safe for you to stay here, Silver Dolphins. There are too many boats moving around. We're going out to sea, and you should go home too."

"We'll be careful," Antonia promised, hiding a smile – Star reminded her of her own mother. "Goodbye."

Antonia and Cai worked their way along the seabed in the opposite direction to the dolphins. They swam slowly, weaving their way through the jungle of boats until at last they were safely out in the open water. Cai swam to the surface and, shielding his eyes with his hand, he stared into the distance.

"Look, there's the minke and her calf."

Antonia looked at the horizon where two small fins were protruding above the water. Sighing contentedly, she said, "I love a happy ending."

"Me too," said Cai quietly.

Suddenly, Antonia felt deflated. If only there was a happy ending for her and Cai. But she couldn't think how to rescue him. If Cai wanted to be a Silver Dolphin, then he'd have to go and live in Australia.

"We'd best get back," she said hoarsely.

They swam home in silence, their bodies arching in time as they dipped in and out of the sea. Leaping along with the sea breeze in her face, Antonia wondered how it was possible that she could feel so happy yet so miserable all at the same time.

Too soon they arrived back at Claudia's beach and as Antonia rose from the sea the water cascaded from her, draining the happiness with it, so she was left with a tangled knot of sadness in her stomach. She paddled ashore, automatically heading for the

Sea Watch boat to get her shoes. But the boat wasn't there.

"We beat Claudia back," said Cai.

"Let's wait for her," said Antonia, grateful for the excuse to prolong the moment before they returned to their normal lives. They sat on the beach watching the sea. A couple of boats came their way, but it was ages before Claudia got back. At first she was just a small dot on the horizon. Gradually the dot grew larger, expanding slowly like a balloon into the Sea Watch boat. The boat chugged closer and, screwing up her eyes, Antonia was able to make out a tall figure sitting in the stern. She waved and Claudia waved back.

"Slowcoach," shouted Cai. "We beat you back by miles."

"I stopped for a chat with Jack," Claudia

answered mildly as the boat reached the shore. "He couldn't believe how many boat owners had answered his call for help. Everyone was amazed when the calf appeared. You did a good job."

Antonia and Cai rolled up their trousers and waded into the sea with the launching trolley. Cutting the engine, Claudia jumped out of the boat and the three of them manoeuvred it on to the trolley then towed it up the beach.

"Phew! Couldn't have done that on my own," said Claudia gratefully.

Cai and Antonia sat on the sand to put on their shoes. Claudia leant against the boat standing on one leg.

"What you did today was incredible," said Claudia as they came off the beach. "You worked so well together."

"Tell that to Mum and Dad," said Cai bitterly.

"I'm going to."

Cai's eyes widened in surprise. "You can't!" he exclaimed. "It's a secret."

"I don't have to tell them *everything*. But I shall say that I couldn't have managed without you."

Chapter Fourteen

hen Claudia opened the kitchen door, Antonia saw Cai's parents sitting at the table with a pile of leaflets spread out in front of them. Both Mr and Mrs Pacific jumped guiltily, then hurriedly collected the leaflets together. Antonia didn't mean to be nosy, but as Mr Pacific slid the leaflets into the dresser drawer

she saw the top one and her stomach turned a somersault. They were house details – the sort you got from an estate agent when you were looking to buy somewhere to live.

Antonia felt crushed with sadness. Couldn't Mr and Mrs Pacific have waited until they got back to Australia before starting to look for a new house?

Claudia reached for the kettle and filled it with water.

"There's tea or squash and there's a chocolate cake in the cupboard. Get it out for me, Cai, and cut yourself and Antonia a nice big slice."

"Not for me," said Antonia hurriedly. She edged to the back door. "I've just remembered, I need to go home early. See you tomorrow."

Claudia stared at her questioningly, but

Antonia closed her mind, not wanting to share her thoughts.

"Can't you stay for a short while?" asked Cai in surprise. "Aunty Claudia will drive you home if you're in a hurry. You don't mind, do you, Aunty?"

"Not at all," said Claudia gallantly.

"Thanks, but I'd better go," said Antonia. "Bye."

She shut the door firmly behind her then ran all the way from Claudia's house to the bottom of Sandy Bay Road before finally stopping to catch her breath. Her heart was hammering against her chest. Checking her watch, Antonia realised that it was much earlier than she'd thought. If she went home now, Mum would ask lots of questions. There were several benches along the road,

looking out to sea. Antonia decided she would sit on one for a while, but then she had a better idea: she'd go round to Sophie's.

Antonia's friend was thrilled to see her.

"Come and help me," she said, pulling Antonia inside. "Dad's holding an exhibition and he said I could show a few of my pictures, but I don't know which ones to pick."

Antonia spent a happy hour with Sophie in her dad's studio going through Sophie's best work. Eventually they chose five pictures, including one of a boat that had been stranded in Sandy Bay and Sophie's latest picture of the whale.

"I need to think of an interesting title for it," said Sophie.

"It's a minke whale," said Antonia helpfully.

"You can tell that just by looking at my picture!" squeaked Sophie. "That means it must be good."

Antonia smiled, thinking of the animal they'd just saved. Being with Sophie cheered Antonia up enormously and she went home with a spring in her step. But as she turned into her road she saw Claudia's car parked on her drive and her mood changed again.

Fearing the worst, Antonia ran the rest of the way and hurriedly went inside. The lounge door was closed, but Antonia could hear adult voices filtering through it. She hesitated. It sounded like Mr and Mrs Pacific talking! Antonia had to find out what was going on. She burst into the lounge and again she saw the same pile of leaflets she'd seen at Claudia's. A red mist crossed in front of

Antonia's eyes. She was so angry she could hear the blood rushing through her ears. Why would Cai's parents bring those details here? Did they really think she was interested in their new *Australian* home?

"There you are," Mrs Lee said, sounding relieved. "What took you so long?"

"I went to see Sophie. I'm not late, am I?" said Antonia defensively.

"No, but when Cai and his parents arrived expecting to find you here, I started to worry," said Mum. "They've come to share some exciting news."

"We've found somewhere to live," said Cai brightly. He snatched a leaflet from his dad and thrust it at Antonia. "Look, isn't it brilliant?"

Reluctantly, Antonia took the leaflet from

Cai. What had got into him? Why was he suddenly so happy about moving?

"It's got an outdoor swimming pool," said Cai enthusiastically. "You can come and swim whenever you want."

"Yeah right!" The words exploded angrily from Antonia. Astonishingly, Mr and Mrs Pacific burst out laughing and so did Cai.

Confused, Antonia stared at the leaflet. It was printed on glossy paper and the house was a pretty cottage. It was nothing like the houses Antonia remembered seeing when she'd visited Australia.

"Where is it?" she asked listlessly. "Is it near the hotel we stayed at?"

Cai clutched his stomach. "N-n-no," he chuckled. "It's on the edge of a place called Sandy Bay."

Antonia narrowed her eyes. It was a coincidence that there was another Sandy Bay in Australia, but it wasn't that funny.

"It's about ten minutes' walk. You still don't get it, do you?" Cai stabbed his finger at the leaflet. "It's *here*. In this Sandy Bay. We're moving here!"

"Cai has really settled here," said Mrs Pacific. "He's so happy and he's made so many good friends. Then there's Sea Watch too – the work he does is amazing. You're both amazing," she added, grinning at Antonia. "The more we thought about it, the crueller it seemed to wrench Cai away from everything he's grown to love and make him start again..."

"So we did some serious thinking," said Mr Pacific, taking over the story. "We're going to

start up our own business letting holiday homes in Sandy Bay. We've discussed our plans with a local estate agent and he thinks he has a house for us to live in and four cottages to let out to tourists. We're going to see the houses tomorrow."

Hot tears welled at the back of Antonia's eyes.

"Well, say something," said Cai.

"Bubbly!" said Antonia.

It was the adults' turn to look confused as Antonia and Cai collapsed with laughter and hugged each other.

When they finally calmed down, Mrs Pacific said, "We're going out tonight to celebrate. Cai tells me there's an Italian restaurant in Sandy Bay and their pizzas are legend. Would you like to come with us to Pepper's Pizzas?"

"Yes, please," said Antonia enthusiastically. "Their pizzas *are* legend."

"That's settled then," said Mrs Pacific. "We'll pick you up at seven."

Antonia waved goodbye to Cai and his parents until their car turned out of sight, then she slipped through the side gate and into the back garden. She stood in the middle of the lawn and stared out to sea. The blue ocean sparkled in the late afternoon sunshine. It was a view that Antonia never grew tired of. This was her home and now it was Cai's home too. Antonia reached for her silver dolphin charm.

"Silver Dolphins forever," she whispered.

And the dolphin twitched its tiny tail in agreement. *Silver Dolphins forever.*

Silver Dolphins

by Summer Waters

OUT NOW!

Silver Dolphins

HIGH TIDE

It's show time in Sandy Bay when a TV filming crew arrives on the beach! But it's hard for Antonia and Cai to answer the call without being noticed. Then a high tide threatens the safety of the crew . . .

Is the Silver Dolphins' secret about to be exposed for good?

HarperCollins *Children's Books*

Silver Dolphins
by Summer Waters

Buy more great Silver Dolphins books from HarperCollins at 10% off recommended retail price. FREE postage and packing in the UK.

Out Now:

Silver Dolphins – The Magic Charm	ISBN: 978-0-00-730968-9
Silver Dolphins – Secret Friends	ISBN: 978-0-00-730969-6
Silver Dolphins – Stolen Treasures	ISBN: 978-0-00-730970-2
Silver Dolphins – Double Danger	ISBN: 978-0-00-730971-9
Silver Dolphins – Broken Promises	ISBN: 978-0-00-730972-6
Silver Dolphins – Moonlight Magic	ISBN: 978-0-00-730973-3
Silver Dolphins – Rising Star	ISBN: 978-0-00-734812-1
Silver Dolphins – Stormy Skies	ISBN: 978-0-00-734813-8
Silver Dolphins – High Tide	ISBN: 978-0-00-736749-8
Silver Dolphins – River Rescue	ISBN: 978-0-00-736750-4

All priced at £4.99

To purchase by Visa/Mastercard/Switch simply call
08707871724 or fax on **08707871725**

To pay by cheque, send a copy of this form with a cheque made payable to
'HarperCollins Publishers' to: Mail Order Dept. (Ref: BOB4),
HarperCollins Publishers, Westerhill Road, Bishopbriggs, G64 2QT,
making sure to include your full name, postal address and phone number.

From time to time HarperCollins may wish to use your personal data
to send you details of other HarperCollins publications and offers.
If you wish to receive information on other HarperCollins publications
and offers please tick this box ☐

Do not send cash or currency. Prices correct at time of press.
Prices and availability are subject to change without notice.
Delivery overseas and to Ireland incurs a £2 per book postage and packing charge.